P9-BJN-829

PLEASANT JOURNEYS

Told by

Pleasant de Spain

storyteller

illustrated by

Kirk Lyttle

for Judith,

Imagine!

Pleasant

The Writing Works, Inc.
Mercer Island, Washington

Gordon Soules Book Publishers
Vancouver, B.C., Canada

Library of Congress Cataloging in Publication Data

DeSpain, Pleasant.
    Pleasant journeys.

    SUMMARY: A collection of 22 folktales from 17
different countries.
    1. Tales. [1. Folklore] I. Lyttle, Kirk.
II. Title.
PZ8.1.D47Pl   398.2   79-5359
ISBN 0-916076-36-9 (v. 1)

Copyright © 1979 by Pleasant deSpain
All Rights Reserved
Manufactured in the United States
Published by The Writing Works, Inc.
                7438 S.E. 40th Street
                Mercer Island, Washington 98040
ISBN: 0-916076-37-7 (U.S.)
Library of Congress Catalog Card Number: 79-5359
Published in Canada by Gordon Soules Book Publishers
    525-355 Burrard Street
    Vancouver, B.C., Canada V6C 2G8
ISBN: 0-919564-37-8 (Canada)

CONTENTS

Acknowledgments

I'm fortunate to have such good and willing
friends and colleagues, and I wish to thank the
following people for their generosity:
Leslie Gillian Abel, Mason Sizemore,
Bob Polishuk, Marilyn Hanna, Merle and Anne Dowd,
Kirk Lyttle, Frank Koontz, and Paul Thompson.

Dedication

for
Robert Guy
a man who listens to his
intuition and acts upon
what he hears. Thanks, Bob.

Tales To Tell

The twenty-two stories in this volume were originally published in "Pleasant Journeys," my weekly column in *The Seattle Times,* during 1977-78, and are my versions of traditional folktales representing seventeen different countries and cultures. The stories were meant to be told, and as a storyteller, I have written them down in much the same way that I tell them.

I am often asked where I find my stories to tell, and my usual response deals with books, other people, and my imagination. But the true source of all my stories is in the telling of them to others, for it is through the process of telling a story over and over again that I'm able to discover its shape, rhythm, mood and, most importantly, its heart.

It is my hope that you will not only read these tales for your own pleasure but that you will also read them aloud to your family and friends, and perhaps even learn and then tell some of them on your own. The world needs more storytellers!

The Turkey and the Fat Mayor

An American Tale

ONCE, a poor old man had a turkey who liked to strut up and down the road. One day, the turkey found a gold nugget as large as your thumb lying in the middle of the road.

"Gobble, gobble, gobble. I'll take this to my hungry master!"

Just as he was heading home with the gold, the mayor happened to walk by. The mayor was fat. In fact, he was *very* fat. A skinny sheriff walked behind him, but you couldn't see him because the mayor was so fat.

When the fat mayor saw the turkey with the gold nugget, he said, "Turkey, I will take that gold home with me."

"No you won't," said the turkey. "It is for my old master, and he needs it more than you."

The fat mayor did not like the word, "No." He spoke to the skinny sheriff, "Get that gold for me!"

The sheriff chased the turkey down the road and took the gold nugget away from him. The mayor took it to his home and put it in his large treasure chest.

The turkey was angry and followed the mayor to his house. Once there, he flew up to a window and called loudly: "Gobble, gobble, gobble, goo. Return my gold, or woe is you!"

The fat mayor became angry and called to the skinny sheriff, "Drown the turkey in the well!"

The sheriff caught the turkey and threw him into the well. But the turkey cried, "Oh empty stomach of mine, drink up the water, and I'll feel fine!"

His stomach drank up all the water and he flew back to the window and cried, "Gobble, gobble, gobble, goo. Return my gold, or woe is you!"

The fat mayor was even angrier than before, and again called to the skinny sheriff: "Throw the turkey into the fireplace and burn him!"

The turkey was caught and thrown into the fireplace. But the turkey said, "Stomach so full, empty the water and save my soul!"

His stomach emptied and the fire went out.

He flew back to the window for a third time and cried, "Gobble, gobble, gobble, goo. Return my gold, or woe is you!"

The fat mayor was as angry as he could be. He called to the skinny sheriff: "Put the turkey on the hill of red ants and let the ants bite him to death!"

The turkey was caught again and placed on the ant hill. The turkey cried, "Oh empty stomach of mine, eat all the red ants, and I'll feel fine!"

His stomach ate up the ants and he flew back to the window and cried, "Gobble, gobble, gobble, goo. Return my gold, or woe is you!"

The fat mayor was so angry that he didn't know what to do with the turkey. He called to the skinny sheriff and asked for his advice.

The sheriff said, "You could pull out all

of his feathers . . . or you could cut off his head . . . or you could sit on him."

"That's just what I'll do!" said the fat mayor. "I'll sit on him! Bring him here!"

The sheriff caught the turkey and brought him to the fat mayor. The mayor placed him on a wide chair and sat down on top of him.

The turkey cried, "Stomach so full, empty the ants and save my soul!"

His stomach emptied and all the red ants began to bite the fat mayor. He jumped up from the chair and yelled, "Yeow, ouch, ohhh, ow! Return the gold nugget to the turkey!"

The skinny sheriff opened the treasure chest.

The turkey looked inside and said, "Oh empty stomach of mine, eat all the treasure, and I'll feel fine!"

His empty stomach ate up all the treasure, and the turkey strutted home. He and his old master lived comfortably ever after.

The Turnip

A Russian Tale

ONE day Grandfather planted a turnip in his garden. It grew and grew and grew, and when it came time to pull it out of the ground, it was huge!

Grandfather pulled and pulled, but he couldn't pull it out of the ground.

"Grandmother, come and help me pull up this turnip!" called Grandfather.

Grandmother pulled on Grandfather and Grandfather pulled on the turnip. They pulled and pulled, but they couldn't pull it out of the ground.

Grandmother called to Mother, "Come and help us pull up this turnip!"

Mother pulled on Grandmother, Grandmother pulled on Grandfather, and Grandfather pulled on the turnip. They pulled and they pulled, but the turnip wouldn't budge.

"Daughter," called Mother, "come and help us pull up this turnip!"

Daughter pulled on Mother, Mother

pulled on Grandmother, Grandmother pulled on Grandfather, and Grandfather pulled on the turnip. They pulled and they pulled, but they couldn't move it.

Daughter called to the dog, "Come and help us pull up this turnip!"

The dog pulled on Daughter, Daughter pulled on Mother, Mother pulled on Grandmother, Grandmother pulled on Grandfather, and Grandfather pulled on the turnip. They pulled and they pulled, but the turnip still wouldn't budge.

The dog barked to the cat, "Come and help us pull up this turnip!"

The cat pulled on the dog, the dog pulled on Daughter, Daughter pulled on Mother, Mother pulled on Grandmother, Grandmother pulled on Grandfather, and Grandfather pulled on the turnip. They pulled and they pulled, but they couldn't pull it out of the ground.

The cat meowed to the mouse, "Come and help us pull up this turnip!"

The mouse pulled on the cat, the cat pulled on the dog, the dog pulled on Daughter, Daughter pulled on Mother, Mother pulled on Grandmother, Grandmother pulled on Grandfather, and Grandfather pulled on the turnip. They pulled and they pulled, but they couldn't pull the turnip out of the ground.

The mouse squeaked to the beetle, "Come and help us pull up this turnip!"

The beetle pulled on the mouse, the mouse pulled on the cat, the cat pulled on the dog, the dog pulled on Daughter, Daughter pulled on Mother, Mother pulled on Grandmother, Grandmother pulled on Grandfather, and Grandfather pulled on the turnip. They pulled and they pulled, and they pulled the huge turnip right up out of the ground!

The turnip was so large that it fell on Grandfather! Grandfather fell on

Grandmother! Grandmother fell on Mother! Mother fell on Daughter! Daughter fell on the dog! The dog fell on the cat! The cat fell on the mouse! The mouse fell on the beetle!

And they all ate the turnip for supper.

Lindy and the Forest Giant

A Swedish Tale

THE Forest Giant lived in a dark cave at the foot of Goat Mountain. He was a lazy and cruel giant who made the inhabitants of the valley below pay a heavy tribute to live in peace.

Once each month, the people had to drive a fat cow to the entrance of the giant's cave and leave it for him to eat. If a valley dweller wanted to fish in the nearby lake, he had to leave a big cheese and one half of his catch for the Forest Giant.

If the people were late with their offerings, or tried to give him less than he demanded, he heaved huge boulders down on their houses and barns and stole their cattle during the night.

Everyone lived in great fear of the giant except for a clever girl named Lindy. Lindy never feared anyone or anything, and one day she decided to make the Forest Giant leave the valley. She picked up her fishing pole and line, and walked to the lake. When she had caught six large trout, she walked up to the giant's cave and yelled inside. "Oh Forest Giant, full of fleas, here's three fish and a cheddar cheese!" And Lindy hurled four rocks into the darkness of the cave.

The giant roared with anger and ran out of the cave. He was so large that he could have swallowed Lindy with one gulp. "How dare you mock me, child! Give me all of your fish or I will step on you!"

Lindy laughed and said, "Be calm, Uncle, and speak softly, or I will have to break your leg."

"But I am much stronger than you," said the giant, "and you are only a little girl."

Now Lindy was angry and her eyes flashed. She pointed to a nearby tree and said, "Very well, Uncle, we will have a contest to determine who is the strongest. Let's see who can make the largest hole in that tree, using only our heads!"

"I'll go first," said the giant, and he ran toward the tree with his head down. He hit the tree so hard that two squirrels were knocked to the ground, but there was no hole in the trunk.

"Ouch!" said the giant, as he rubbed his head. "I will try again!" This time he crashed into the tree so hard that the whole valley shook. The giant fell to the ground in a heap, as he had knocked himself out.

Lindy quickly pulled some of the bark off the tree and chopped a hole in the trunk, large enough to put her head through. Then she placed the bark back over the hole.

The giant woke up and said that his head was too sore to try again.

"Are you so weak, Uncle?" asked Lindy. "Let me have a turn and show you how it's done." She rammed into the bark where she had made the hole, and her head came out of the other side.

The giant, amazed at Lindy's strength, said, "You may fish in the lake without paying me."

"Listen, Uncle," said Lindy, "Pay me

for all of the cattle, fish and cheese that you have taken from the villagers, or I will squeeze you in half!"

"Come into my cave and we will have some supper," replied the giant. "I will give you the money in the morning."

Lindy realized that the giant would try to kill her during the night, so she waited until he had eaten a huge plateful of fish and lay down to sleep. When he was snoring loudly, she crept out of the cave and found a small log. She carried the log back inside, covered it with a blanket, and then hid behind a rock in the cave's darkest corner.

Soon after, the giant awoke. He picked up his axe and gave the log a heavy blow, thinking that it was Lindy under the blanket. Then he lay back down and started to snore once again.

Lindy quickly tossed the log outside the cave. Then she lay down, pulled the blanket over her, and waited until morning.

When the giant opened his eyes and saw that she wasn't hurt, he became frightened and started to stutter. "DDDDid youuuu ssssleep wwwell?"

"Oh yes," said Lindy, "except for the little mosquito that bit me during the night. Now I'll take the money that you owe me."

The Forest Giant gave her a large bag of silver coins, and because he was afraid of Lindy's terrible strength, he moved away from Goat Mountain.

The villagers lived in peace forever after.

Lord Bag of Rice

A Japanese Tale

ONCE long ago in old Japan, a brave soldier started to cross a bridge and saw a huge black snake coiled on the wooden planks. The man walked up to the snake and stepped on its head. Instantly the snake was gone and the Dwarf-King stood before the astonished soldier.

"At last I have found a brave man!" cried the dwarf. "I have waited here for three days for someone strong-hearted enough to help me, but everyone turned and ran when they saw the snake. Will you help to save many lives?"

The soldier replied, "I serve the Emperor and believe in righting that which is wrong. What is your trouble?"

"A giant centipede lives on the mountain, and each day he comes to this lake to drink. He washes his thousand filthy feet in the pure water, turning it poisonous and foul. The fish die and so do the other animals that come to drink from the lake.

"I am willing to help," said the brave soldier.

The Dwarf-King said a magic word and the soldier found himself in a palace at the bottom of the lake. It was a glorious palace with beautiful rooms made of pearl, silver and gold. Mermaids served them fresh fruit and green tea, while a school of goldfish sang sweet melodies.

Just then they heard a loud rumble and a mighty roar! It felt like an earthquake!

"He's coming!" cried the dwarf. "His thousand heavy feet are marching down the mountain. We must stop him from poisoning the water!"

A moment later they were at the edge of the lake and could see the giant centipede. He looked like a brightly colored dragon, with far too many legs, moving rapidly down the steep slope of the mountain towards the clear blue lake.

The soldier was a skillful archer. He drew his great bow and carefully aimed at the demon. The arrow flew through the air and struck the centipede on the head, but then fell away without hurting him. The second arrow found its mark as well, but it too, fell away. As the monster approached the water's edge, the soldier drew his last arrow.

Suddenly he remembered what his father had told him when he was a boy— if you spit on the arrowhead, it will kill any creature, no matter how large or terrible.

In a flash he spit and sent the arrow flying! It struck the centipede in the head and the monster fell to the ground, dead.

Then the soldier felt very drowsy, and he lay down to rest. When he awoke he found himself back in his own house, which was now changed into a magnificent castle. He also found three gifts given to him by the Dwarf-King.

First, there was a large bell made of bronze. The story of the battle with the centipede was told in pictures on the outside of the bell. The second gift was a sword which would always bring victory to its owner.

The third was the best gift of all. It was a bag of rice which always stayed full, even though he drew rice from it for himself and his friends for years and years.

It was because of this gift that the people called him, "Lord Bag of Rice."

Reynard and the Fisherman

A French Tale

MONSIEUR Reynard-the-Fox walked down to the river and decided to have fish for his supper. Since he lived by his tricks alone, Reynard walked until he came to an old fisherman putting his pole and worms into his cart. A long string of fat fish hung from his belt.

"That is my supper for tonight," thought Reynard.

The fisherman placed the fish in the back of his cart, and climbed up to the seat. "Get up, Gigi," he said to the horse. "I want to be home before dark."

The fox trotted along the river bank, being careful to stay hidden in the trees. When he was far enough ahead of the fisherman's slow-moving cart, he lay on his back in the middle of the road, with his feet pointing to the sky. He lay very still, his mouth open and his eyes closed.

Soon, the horse pulled the cart up to the fox and stopped.

"Gigi, why have you stopped? It is late and we must get home," said the fisherman.

But Gigi wouldn't budge, and the old man had to climb down from his seat to see what was wrong. His eyes opened wide when he saw Monsieur Reynard-the-Fox lying there.

"What's this? The tricky fox is dead? Wonderful! Now my chickens are safe. And his red fur will bring a high price at market. What a fortunate day!"

He placed the fox in the back of the cart, next to the fish, and started on his way once again.

"When I sell the fox's fur," said the happy fisherman, "I'll use the money to buy a cow. The cow will have a calf and then I will be twice as rich. I'll sell them both and buy a small flock of sheep."

Reynard licked his chops and began to eat the fish.

"And then," continued the fisherman, "the sheep will have lambs. I can sell them and buy a new house. I'll turn the house into an inn and make so much money that I'll be able to buy the biggest store in town!"

Reynard swallowed another fat fish.

"So many people will shop at my store that I will soon be as rich as the king. Of course, I'll have to build a magnificent castle! I'll never have to fish again because I'll have one hundred servants and fifty cooks. I will eat wonderful meals from gold and silver plates!"

Reynard ate the last fish and stood up. "Mr. Fisherman," he said, "since I have helped you become so rich, I trust that you will invite me to share your kingly spread."

The fisherman turned around. "But . . . but . . . but you're dead!"

"Then I must run home and tell my old mother. She will be very sad to hear it."

The fox leaped from the cart and started to run into the woods.

"Stop!" cried the fisherman. "I must have your fur. Without it, I will have nothing!"

Reynard kept running.

"Thief! Thief!" yelled the fisherman. "You are robbing me of my castle and my servants!"

The fox shouted back, "And I thought that I was only robbing you of your fish!"

With a sly grin and a full stomach, Monsieur Reynard-the-Fox ran home to his den.

27

The Silly Farmer

An Ethiopian Tale

ONCE there was a silly farmer named Zaheed. One day his wife told him that she was going to have a baby. Zaheed asked her what kind of baby it would be, but she didn't know.

"Then," said Zaheed, "I will visit the wise old woman who lives at the base of the mountains. She has magic, both black and white, and she will be able to tell me."

He took a gold piece that he had hidden deep in his mattress and walked all morning until he reached the old witch's hut.

"I've come to ask you a difficult question," said Zaheed. "And if you can give me a satisfactory answer, I'll pay you with this piece of gold."

The old woman stared at him with dark eyes and nodded her agreement.

"My wife is going to have a child, but she doesn't know what kind it will be. Can you tell me!"

The old woman opened a small wooden chest and removed three ancient bones. She tossed them on the ground and studied the pattern they made. She shook her head and said, "Ehh."

Zaheed shook his head and said, "Ehh."

She tossed them again and studied the pattern. "Ahh!"

"Ahh!" repeated Zaheed.

Once more she tossed the bones and studied the pattern. "Of course!" she exclaimed.

"Of course!" shouted Zaheed.

"Your wife's child will be either a boy or a girl."

"How wonderful!" said Zaheed. He gave the witch the gold piece and ran home to tell his wife the good news.

Several months later his wife had a fat baby girl. "You see," Zaheed told all of his neighbors, "the old woman was right!"

Soon it was time to baptise the girl, but Zaheed and his wife couldn't think of a proper name for her.

"I'll go ask the old woman," said Zaheed. "She is wise and will tell me our daughter's name."

He took another piece of gold from the mattress and walked back to the witch's hut. After Zaheed explained the problem, the old woman took the bones from the chest and tossed them onto the floor. "Ahh!" said she.

"Ahh!" said Zaheed.

Again she tossed the bones. "Of course!"

"Of course!" repeated Zaheed.

"Give me the gold," said the witch, "and I will whisper the child's name into your hands."

Zaheed did as she said and extended his hands. She quickly whispered into them and said, "Now close your hands tight so that you won't lose it on the way home."

The farmer ran toward home with his hands clasped together. When he came to his neighbor's farm he saw several of the men pitching hay into tall stacks. "I have it! I have it!" he cried. "The name of my daughter is here in my hands!"

Just then he slipped on some loose hay

and fell to the ground. His hands came apart, and he yelled, "Now I've lost it! Quickly, help me find it again!"

Several of the men ran up and helped Zaheed search through the haystack with their pitchforks.

Soon after, a woman from the village walked by and asked what they were looking for. Zaheed explained how the witch had given him the name and how he had lost it.

"It is nonsense!" she declared, "Simply nonsense!"

"Oh, thank you!" said Zaheed. "I thought I had lost it forever."

When he got home the silly farmer explained everything to his wife. "The witch whispered the name into my hands, but I lost it on the way home. The neighbor woman found it and told it to me. Our daughter's name is Nonsense! Simply Nonsense!"

And they call her Simply Nonsense, to this very day.

The Dancing Wolves

An American Tale

ONCE, a rabbit walked through the woods on his way to visit the woodchuck. The woodchuck was his best friend and lived in a cozy hole under an old tree stump.

The rabbit was so pleased with the thought of his visit, that he wasn't being careful to stay hidden in the brush and bushes. Suddenly, seven large and hungry wolves leaped out from behind seven trees and surrounded the rabbit.

"Rabbit," said one, "we are going to eat you for lunch!"

The rabbit was frightened, but he kept his wits and said, "But all of you can't eat me. I'm just a little fellow, only a mouthful. I agree that one of you should have me, but which one?"

The wolves began to argue among themselves, each claiming the rabbit.

"Stop!" said the rabbit. "I have thought of an idea which will solve the problem. Do you like to dance?"

"We love to dance!" said the wolves.

"Then let me teach you a new dance, and whoever dances best will win me for the prize!"

The wolves agreed and the rabbit

described the dance.

"Since there are seven of you, the dance is in seven parts. First, you line up, one behind the other. I'll stand by this tree and sing, and you dance away from me until I yell, 'Turn!' Then you turn around and dance back. But stay in line!"

"We will! We will!" shouted the wolves.

The rabbit sang:

"Dance, dance, dance,
Each has a chance.
Yum, yum, yum,
Rabbit in my tum."

The wolves danced away from him and kept their line straight. When the rabbit yelled, "Turn!," the wolves danced back and encircled him.

"Wonderful!" said the rabbit. "How beautifully you dance! For the second part, I sing from that other tall tree over there and you dance as before, except that on every seventh step, you turn one complete circle, and chant 'Tibbar! Tibbar!' "

(Which is really "Rabbit! Rabbit!" spelled backwards.)

"This is fun!" cried the wolves.

The rabbit ran to the tall tree and sang his little song:

"Dance, dance, dance,
Each has a chance.
Yum, yum, yum,
Rabbit in my tum."

And the wolves did their dancing and turning and chanting. When the rabbit yelled, "Turn!," they danced back to him.

"Magnificent!" said the rabbit as he ran to the next tall tree. "That was much better than before! Now for the third part. Again you dance away from me, but this time you add a hop to every third step, clap your paws on every fifth step, and keep the turnaround on every seventh step."

And so it went, the rabbit moving from

tree to tree with each part of the dance, and in doing so, getting closer and closer to the woodchuck's hole. The wolves had to concentrate harder and harder as each new dance became more complicated, and had nearly forgotten about eating the rabbit.

When it was time for the seventh dance, the rabbit had moved quite close to the woodchuck's hole.

The rabbit said, "This is the last dance, and it is the most fun! It is a racing dance and you must run away from me as fast as you can and turn a somersault on every tenth step. When I stop singing, and yell, 'Turn!' you all race back. The first one to reach me gets me for lunch!"

The rabbit sang:
"Rabbit for lunch!
But I have a hunch,
Whoever gets here first,
Will eat leaves and dirt!"

"Rabbit for lunch!" shouted the wolves, and away they ran, turning somersaults on every tenth step.

After the wolves were a good distance away, the rabbit yelled "Turn!," and made a quick dash for the woodchuck's hole.

The wolves raced back, each one hungry for the rabbit. The rabbit, however, had vanished from sight.

Then, from under the ground, the wolves heard the last of rabbit's songs:
"Wolves can dance,
Wolves can prance
And do funny things,
When rabbit sings!"

The Magic Purse

An Irish Tale

ONCE a young Irishman named Mike O'Hara spied a small man all dressed in green, sitting in the shade of a large toadstool at the edge of the forest. Mike immediately recognized that this was a leprechaun. He had always hoped to catch one, because he knew that leprechauns carry a magic purse with a single shilling inside. Each time the shilling is removed another one appears, and thus the purse is never empty.

Now Mike was a lazy sort of man who hated to work and he thought that his dream of a rich and easy life was about to come true. He crept up to the wee man as quietly as a mouse, grabbed him about the waist and held him tight.

"Now I've got you, my little friend, and you had better give me your magic purse or you'll not live to see the sun rise in the morning sky."

"But I'm no leprechaun and I have no purse!" cried the little man.

"Your purse or your life," replied Mike, "and I'll give you but one minute more to decide."

The leprechaun, for that indeed was what he was, reluctantly reached inside his green jacket and pulled out a beautiful purse made of red silk. Then he carefully opened it to show Mike the single shilling inside.

Mike grabbed the purse and set the leprechaun on the ground. The wee man laughed once and then vanished.

Mike was as pleased as he could be with his new-found purse and as soon as he got back to town he went to the inn and ordered drinks for everyone.

"Where's your money, Mike O'Hara?" asked Mrs. McCarthy, the owner of the inn. She was suspicious because it was a well-known fact that Mike was always broke.

"Right here in me pocket," said Mike. "I'm a rich man now, and never again will I have to work. Come lads, let's quench our thirst with some good Irish whiskey!"

They drank until the bottle was dry and then Mike called for a grand feast for himself and all of his friends.

"Not until you pay me in cash for the whiskey already gone," said Mrs. McCarthy.

"Right you are," said Mike, and he took the silk purse from his pocket and told them all about his encounter with the leprechaun. "And," he concluded, "every time I take a shilling out of the magic purse another one appears. Watch."

And hey presto! He pulled the shilling out and . . . the next shilling failed to appear . . . the purse was empty.

(Now it is not as well known, but leprechauns carry two silk purses, one magic and one ordinary, in case they get caught.)

Mike turned red with anger and embarrassment when he realized that he had been tricked. And to make matters worse, he had but one shilling with which to pay for an expensive bottle of whiskey.

"Tell us again about your leprechaun!" laughed the other men.

Mrs. McCarthy called for a policeman and had Mike arrested. Mike told the judge that he had been tricked by the leprechaun, and pleaded for mercy.

The judge frowned and said, "I will believe your story only if you produce the leprechaun and he verifies it. Otherwise, thirty days of hard labor!"

Mike O'Hara did his time and never again did he try to catch a leprechaun.

The Man Who Was on Fire Behind

A Swiss Tale

ONCE there was a man named William who liked to play tricks on his neighbors. On more than one occasion his neighbors returned home to find their chickens locked in the clothes closet or their goats up on the roof. One neighbor even found a goldfish in his drinking water!

In the next village there lived a clever young woman named Greta. One afternoon, while she was preparing dinner, William knocked on her door and asked for a drink of water. Greta recognized him at once and said, "Of course. Come in and rest yourself by the warm fire, while I go to the well and fetch a fresh bucket." She didn't let on that she knew who he was, but the people of her village often laughed at William's pranks.

While she was gone, William examined everything in the kitchen. He felt the bread dough rising in the pans on the window sill; he peeked into the tall cookie jar and helped himself to a fresh oatmeal cookie; and he lifted the lid from the large black kettle hanging over the burning logs in the fireplace. A delicious odor rose from inside the pot and tickled his nose. Thick chunks of beef were browning nicely for Greta's supper.

William quickly stabbed the largest chunk of meat and put it into his knapsack, which lay on the floor.

When Greta returned with the water she noticed that a faint wisp of steam carrying the odor of cooked beef escaped from the knapsack. She thought for a moment and said, "Now, kind friend, I must ask a favor of you. I need more wood for my fire. Please carry an armload in from the woodshed."

William agreed. While he was gone, Greta took the beef from his knapsack and plopped it back into the kettle. Then she took a smouldering piece of wood from the fire and stuffed it into the leather sack.

William returned with the wood and was anxious to be on his way. He quickly threw the knapsack over his shoulder and started walking toward his village.

"The beef is still good and hot," he said to himself. "I can feel it on my back, right through the leather. How tasty it will be!" The piece of burning wood grew hotter and hotter, and William began to run. As he got close to home, his back seemed to be on fire!

Two neighbors yelled at him as he passed by, "Hey, William, what is that smoking on your back!?"

"My dinner!" he replied.

"Your dinner has set you on fire behind!" the neighbors laughed. "And it has burned the back of your coat and the seat of your pants!"

William ran for the nearest duck pond and jumped in. The water hissed and steamed as a white mist rose from his backside.

For many weeks to follow, the villagers teased him by saying, "Hey, William, are you on fire behind?"

He had learned his lesson, and never again did William play tricks on his neighbors.

The Horse and the Dog

An American Tale

MARTIN was an honest but poor man who owned very little in this world. His only possessions were a strong horse and and old dog. He loved both of the animals and was often heard to say that he couldn't live without them.

One morning Martin went out to feed the horse and found that he was gone. He looked all over the countryside for him, but to no avail. It seemed as though the horse had vanished from the face of the earth.

"My good horse must be lost in the wilderness," said Martin, "with no one to feed him oats and hay. How I would love to see his brown eyes and hear his happy neigh once more. I wouldn't want to keep him; oh no, I would just like to see that he is all right. In fact, I would sell him for one dollar if only I could see him once again."

Just then Martin heard a familiar neigh. He looked up and saw something coming towards him in the distance. It looked like a man and a horse. The man was old and grey, and the horse was . . . was . . . his . . . horse! Martin ran to the horse and hugged him around the neck.

"Where did you find him?" he asked the old man.

"In my field. He was hungry and I fed him. I've been searching for his owner and I suppose that is you."

"I shall always be grateful to you," replied Martin happily.

That night Martin remembered his promise to sell the horse for one dollar if he could but see him again. Since he was an honest man, he knew that he would have to keep his promise. But it was not an easy thing to do and he thought about it long into the night.

The next morning he rode the horse to town. The old dog followed behind. When he got to the livery stable he said in a loud voice, "I want to sell my horse, and a fine animal he is!"

"How much do you want for him?" asked one of several men who gathered around.

"One dollar," answered Martin.

"Only one dollar?" someone asked. "Is that all? Just one dollar for this good horse? You must be mad."

"Well," said Martin, "I know that one dollar seems like a low price, but I also want to sell my old dog for one hundred dollars, and I will only sell my horse to the man who buys my dog. Now then, who will be the first to give me one hundred dollars for my dog and one dollar for my horse?"

The men who wanted to buy the horse became angry. "One hundred dollars for an old dog! That is ridiculous!"

"You cannot have the horse without the dog," said Martin. "Will anyone buy both?"

He waited for a short time longer and then said, "I have tried to keep my promise to sell my horse for one dollar, but can I help it if no one will buy him?"

Martin rode his horse back home and the old dog followed behind.

All three lived happily together for the rest of their days.

The Three Wishes

A Swedish Tale

ONCE a poor woodcutter went to the forest to chop down trees. Just as he raised his stout axe to a large old pine, a wood nymph called down from a high branch.

"Please don't harm this tree. It is my home!"

"Very well," said the man, and he lowered the axe.

"Thank you, woodcutter," said the nymph, "and because you are such a decent fellow, your next three wishes will be answered."

The woodcutter worked hard the rest of the day and was hungry by the time he arrived at his humble cottage. Since he really didn't believe in magic, he had forgotten about the wood nymph's wishes.

He sat at the table and his wife placed a bowl of weak broth and a hard crust of brown bread in front of him.

"What? Is this all there is for my supper? How I wish I had a nice fat sausage to eat with it," said he.

As soon as the words were spoken, a large sausage appeared on his plate.

"Bless my soul!" cried his wife. "Where did that come from?"

Then the woodcutter remembered what

the wood nymph had said about the three wishes, and he told his wife what had happened in the forest that morning.

"And now you've wasted a perfectly good wish on a sausage! You are the most foolish man I've ever heard of. You know how much we need a nicer cottage, and a team of horses, and money to pay taxes with! And what do you wish for? A sausage, a stupid sausage, that's what you wish for!"

"How you go on about it," said the woodcutter. "I wish the sausage would stick to your nose!"

The sausage flew up from the plate and landed on the end of the wife's nose. She tried to pull it off, but it wouldn't budge.

Her husband tried, too, but no matter how hard he pulled, it wouldn't come off.

"Hurry and use your last wish to get it off," said the wife. "I can't stand to have such a long nose."

"But what about our new cottage and all the money we need? Wouldn't it be better to have those things?"

His wife shook her head no, and looked so unhappy with the long sausage hanging down from her nose, that the woodcutter said: "Then don't you ever say I wasted the last wish. I wish the sausage gone!"

It vanished in an instant, and with it, so did all the riches the two of them might have had.

The Jackal and the Tiger

A Tibetan Tale

ONCE a family of jackals traveled through the jungle in search of a new home. They came upon a tiger's den and the father jackal peered cautiously inside. He found that the tiger was gone, but had left behind the hindquarter of a freshly killed deer.

Mr. Jackal took his family inside and they had a fine meal. Then he explained to his wife and children:

"Since I know how to deal with tigers, you may all go to sleep. I will be outside the cave and keep a lookout for the tiger. When he returns I'll growl twice. You, dear wife, must wake up the children and have them cry. I will then ask you why they are crying and you must explain that it is time for their supper."

The young jackals and their mother lay down to sleep in the cave while their father climbed up on a large rock near the cave's entrance. Soon after, he heard the cracking of twigs deep in the jungle and realized that the tiger was returning home. Mr. Jackal growled twice and Mrs. Jackal woke the little jackals and told them to start crying.

"Why are those children crying?"

demanded Mr. Jackal in a loud voice.

"They are very hungry and want their supper," called Mrs. Jackal.

"Tell them to be patient," said Mr. Jackal. "We shall all be enjoying delicious tiger meat before long."

The tiger heard every word and became frightened. "A fierce animal of some kind waits for me in my own den with plans to feed me to his family! I must run away while I can."

And off he ran through the jungle until he came to a large tree. An old monkey sat high in the branches and called to the tiger. "What are you running from, friend?"

The tiger explained what had happened and the monkey began to laugh.

"How silly you are!" explained the monkey. That wasn't a ferocious beast in your den, it was only a jackal. Tigers eat jackals; jackals don't eat tigers! I will return to your den with you and show you how to handle a jackal."

"But I'm still a little frightened," said the tiger. "And how do I know that you won't run away and leave me all alone at the den?"

"We will tie our tails together with a vine," explained the monkey, "and then I cannot leave your side."

With their tails lashed together, they walked cautiously back to the cave. The tiger was quite nervous and ready to flee at any moment.

When Mr. Jackal heard and then saw them approaching with their tails tied together, he called out in his loudest voice, "Excellent, friend monkey, bring him right up to the den. We are all starved for fresh tiger meat. But why did you bring just one tiger? You said that you would bring two!"

The tiger thought that the monkey had

tricked him and was leading him into a trap. He leaped into the air and bounded into the deepest part of the jungle as fast as he could go! The poor monkey was dragged, bumped, and jerked along behind until the end of his long tail finally broke off.

From that night forth, the family of jackals lived comfortably in the den as the tiger was much too afraid to return.

The Golden Pitcher

A Mongolian Tale

THERE once was a king who feared growing old for he thought that old age was a sign of weakness.

"If I grow old," he thought, "my people will neither respect nor fear me. I must remove all traces of old age from my kingdom!"

Thus he commanded that every old person be either banished from the kingdom or slain.

With tears in their eyes and sorrow upon their hearts, the young people helped their parents and grandparents pack up their belongings in order to leave the country in which they had lived for so long.

The king then took precautions to hide his own impending age. He dyed his hair to hide the gray, and put heavy makeup on his face to cover the wrinkles.

Each day, the youth of the kingdom came to beg the king's mercy to allow their parents to return. Growing tired of their lamentations, he finally issued a new decree:

"Whoever finds the golden pitcher at the bottom of the lake will be allowed to bring their parents home; but whoever tries and fails, will forfeit all his land to the king."

Several adventurous youths and strong-hearted maidens ran to the bank of the deep lake. The clear water shimmered in the sunlight and the golden pitcher could be seen resting on the bottom. It was tall and slender with a curved handle.

The young people dove into the warm water, but all failed to bring the pitcher to the surface. Thus the cruel king grew even more rich with the confiscation of their lands.

At this time there was a young woman named Lillith, who loved her old father more than anything in the world. She had hidden him in a mountain cave when the king's order of banishment was issued, and each day she would sneak to the hiding place to bring him food.

One day, she said to her father, "I am troubled by the king's pitcher. Why is it that when I look into the water I can see it clearly, but when anyone dives for it, they return empty-handed?"

Her father thought about this for several minutes and then asked, "Is there a tree on the bank of the lake?"

"Yes, Father, a large elm."

"And can the pitcher be seen in the shadow of the tree?"

"Yes," said Lillith, "the shadow of the tree spreads halfway across the lake, and the pitcher can be seen in that shadow."

The old man nodded and said, "You will find the golden pitcher in the branches of the tree. The pitcher that you see in the water is only its reflection.

Lillith ran to the king and said that she would bring the pitcher from the bottom of the lake.

"Very well," said the king. "I will enjoy adding your land to my holdings."

The king ordered his coach and rode

with Lillith to the lake. Several of the townspeople ran on ahead so that they could watch the dive.

When all were assembled, Lillith began to climb the spreading elm that grew from the bank. The people thought that she was going to dive from one of the low-hanging branches, but instead she climbed to the very top!

It was there that she found the golden pitcher with the curved handle. It hung upside down so that in its reflection, it seemed to stand right side up on the bottom of the lake. She climbed down from the tree and presented it to the king.

"How did you solve this puzzle?" demanded the king.

"My old father, whom I have hidden from you, discovered the answer."

"Well," said the king, "Where fifty youths failed, one old man succeeded. The wisdom that comes with age is valuable after all!"

From that day forth, old age was respected in that country.

The Shoemaker and the Elves

A German Tale

THERE was once a poor shoemaker who had nothing left but enough leather to make one pair of shoes. That night he cut the leather into proper-sized pieces and left them on his workbench, all ready to be sewn together.

In the morning, to his great amazement, he found that the shoes were already made. And what beautiful shoes they were! Each stitch was so carefully placed that the work had to have been done by a master craftsman. Just then a customer entered the shop and tried the shoes on. They fit him perfectly and he paid a good price for them.

Now the shoemaker had enough money to buy leather for two pairs of shoes. He cut them out that night and left them on his workbench, ready to be sewn the next morning. But when he awoke, he found them beautifully finished, just as before. Two customers entered his shop and gave him enough money to purchase leather for four pairs of shoes. He cut them out and left them on the workbench. The next morning the shoes were again ready to be sold.

Several customers were waiting at his

door as news of the wonderful shoes had spread throughout the town, and each tried to outbid the other for a pair. The shoemaker made enough money to buy leather for twenty pairs of shoes, and spent all of that day cutting them out. In the morning, twenty pairs of shoes, all stitched together and looking handsome, sat on his workbench. Again, a large crowd of people waited to buy them.

And so it went. He cut the leather out each night and the shoes were ready to be sold each morning. Soon he was a rich man.

One night, during the month of December, the shoemaker said to his wife, "Let's stay awake tonight and see who comes to help us."

They left a candle burning on the workbench, and hid behind the clothes in a nearby closet. As the clock struck twelve, the door to the shop opened as if by magic, and two tiny men, as naked as on the day they were born, ran into the room. The shoemaker's mouth dropped open as he and his wife watched the elves climb up to the workbench and set to work. They hammered and stitched so rapidly that the work was done in a few moments! Then they climbed down from the bench and ran out of the shop and into the night.

The next morning the shoemaker's wife said, "Husband, those nice little men have made our fortune and we should do something for them. Now here it is, the dead of winter and as cold as it can be, and they don't have even a stitch of clothing, poor souls. I'll make them each a shirt, coat and vest, and a nice pair of trousers. You can make shoes for them."

The shoemaker agreed.

On the night when everything was ready, they placed the gifts on the workbench, and again hid in the closet.

When the clock struck twelve, the door opened and in ran the two naked elves. They climbed up to the workbench and instead of leather pieces, they saw the fine clothes and shoes, just their size! They quickly put them on and began to dance around and around singing:

"How dandy we look in our coats and our vests!

No more will we work for now we can rest!"

They danced out the door and never came again, but from that time forth, the shoemaker had a thriving business.

Christina's Christmas Garden

A Scandinavian Tale

YOUNG Christina lived in the deepest part of the forest with her old mother. They were so poor that all the children who lived in the village called them, "Beggar Girl" and "Beggar Mother."

Christina and her mother lived in a cave carved out of the side of a mountain wall. A crude door of boughs and branches kept the cold winds out as best it could. There were smooth stones for the floor, and Beggar Mother cooked their simple meals in an iron pot that hung over the fire pit. They slept on beds of straw, and for clothing they wore the skins of animals.

"Beggar Girl looks like a bear!
Beggar Girl runs like a hare!"
chanted the village children whenever they saw Christina.

She had been scorned by the villagers all of her life, but she wasn't bitter or angry. The whole forest knew that she was loving and kind.

Whenever her mother returned with a loaf of dry bread, which she had begged from the people in the village, Christina would spread a few crumbs on the ground for the birds and squirrels. She knew where to find wild berries and sweet honey and she knew which trees dropped the best nuts. She could dig for roots and she often found wild onions. She carried cold spring water to the cave each day and she always played gentle games with the wild animals.

Now it was winter and the cold forest slept under a heavy blanket of snow.

Christina looked into the windows of the villager's homes and knew that it was Christmas Eve. Hearty meals were set on tables and colorful gifts were piled high under candlelit Christmas trees. Families gathered around warm fireplaces to sing songs of peace and goodwill, but when they saw Beggar Girl peeking into their festivities, they chased her away with angry words. She belonged to the forest; not to them.

Christina walked through the snow until she came to the little church on the edge of the village. Old Brother Peter cared for the church. He had trimmed the pews with pine boughs, and was ready to ring the big iron bell that hung in the belfry. The rope was frozen stiff, however, and he hadn't the strength to make it ring.

Christina liked Brother Peter and she often brought him dead branches from the forest to warm his winter fire.

In spite of the blinding snow, the small girl quickly climbed up to the belfry and yanked on the frozen rope once, twice, three times! The ice-covered bell began to ring and crisp, loud notes announced Christmas Eve.

And something wonderful began to happen. As Christina rang the bell, the snow melted and the forest turned green. Flowers of every color sprang up from the earth and the bees and butterflies danced in the air. Birds, squirrels, rabbits and chipmunks appeared, and their happy songs and chatterings broke the once cold silence.

Sweet strawberries and plump blackberries ripened on tangled vines, and in the distance the bubbling of the brook could be clearly heard. A warm sun poured light and life into the darkest corner of the forest, and white doves circled on quiet wings.

The villagers ran from their houses and watched with wonder as Christina climbed down the steep steps of the belfry tower and started to walk home. Flowers bloomed wherever she stepped and butterflies fluttered happily above her head. The girl laughed for joy and the villagers, feeling her joy, laughed with her. The entire forest had become Christina's Christmas garden.

The next morning, however, the forest was covered with a fresh blanket of snow, for it had to return to its cold, winter sleep.

St. Stanislaw and the Wolf

A Polish Tale

ONCE long ago in Poland, when animals still used human speech, a holy man named St. Stanislaw lived in the forest. The Saint loved all animals, and he was so compassionate that even the wildest of creatures would come to talk with him. St. Stanislaw listened patiently and always gave good advice, and thus the animals grew to love and trust him.

One morning a large wolf approached the holy man and said, "Good morning, friend."

"And a glorious good morning to you," replied St. Stanislaw.

"I have a problem and I need your advice, kind Saint."

"What is the problem, dear wolf?"

"Human meat," said the wolf. "I've eaten every kind of meat available in the land—rabbit, goat, horse, deer, cow and chicken, but I've never eaten human meat, and the bear says that it is best of all because it is tender and juicy."

"The bear is only kidding you," said the Saint. "Human meat is actually quite tough and dry. You wouldn't like it at all."

"But I must find out for myself, great Saint. Please let me eat a human. I'll only do it once, I promise."

Realizing that the wolf would do it with or without his permission, the Saint said, "Very well, you may eat one human, but you must not eat a young or an old person. The only one that you can eat is a blacksmith. Agreed?"

"Agreed!" said the hungry wolf, and he ran through the forest until he came to the road. There he waited for a blacksmith.

Before long a child on his way to school came by.

"Who are you?" asked the wolf.

"I am a school boy and this is my lunch box. Do you want an apple?"

"No," said the wolf. "I am waiting for someone else. You go on to school."

Soon an old woman walked by.

The wolf's empty stomach grumbled as he asked, "Who are you?"

"I am an old woman as you can tell by my white hair. I'm going to the village to buy food. If you are still here when I return, I'll give you a nice lump of sugar."

"Then off to the village with you," said the wolf.

Shortly after that a strong young blacksmith wearing a leather apron came along.

The wolf ground his teeth in anticipation and asked, "Who are you?"

"I am the village blacksmith, friend wolf. Why do you ask?"

"Because St. Stanislaw gave me permission to eat your tender and juicy flesh."

The blacksmith, whose hands and face were covered with soot, said, "I'll taste better if I'm clean. Allow me to wash myself in the river before you eat me."

"Very well," said the wolf, "but hurry, for I am hungry."

The bold young man walked through the trees on his way to the river and found a thick branch shaped like a club lying on the ground. He hid the club in his jacket and then washed his hands and face. Upon returning he asked if he could dry his wet hands on the wolf's bushy tail.

The wolf agreed and turned around. Immediately the blacksmith grabbed the tail with his strong fist and held tight. Then he pulled the club from his jacket and beat the wolf so hard that he was knocked unconcious. The blacksmith then continued on his journey to town.

When he came to, the poor wolf dragged his bleeding body back to St. Stanislaw's forest hut. The wolf was badly bruised and every muscle ached. When he saw the Saint he cried, "You were right as always. Human meat is tough and dry. Never again do I want to taste it."

"Come my friend," said the gentle Saint, "let me clean and bind your wounds."

The Hungry Fox

A Jewish Tale

ONCE there was a fox who always wanted more of everything. One day while out looking for food, he came to the home of a wealthy merchant. The house was as large as a palace and a thick wall surrounded the beautiful garden in the back. The finest fruit in all of Jerusalem grew in abundance in the garden, and the sly fox wanted his share.

He walked slowly around the outside of the garden looking for a way in, when at last he saw a small hole in the wall. Unfortunately the hole was too small for a fat fox to wiggle through.

The fox looked up longingly at the fruit trees behind the sturdy wall. His eyes widened when he saw the ripe golden pears and fuzzy red peaches just waiting to be eaten; his mouth watered when he spied the delicious apples and abundant cherries; and his stomach growled as he stared at the sweet grapes that hung heavy on the vines.

"There must be some way for me to get through that hole," said the hungry fox. He was able to stick his head through, but his body was simply too large to follow. He began to pace back and forth in front of the wall, trying to find a solution to his problem. "If only I could squeeze through the hole."

Then the fox had an idea. "I will fast until my body is as narrow as my head. I will eat nothing for five days and then, once inside, I'll enjoy a good feast!"

And thus he starved himself for five long and very hungry days. At last he was skinny, so skinny in fact, that he was able to wiggle through the small hole.

Then his sumptuous feast began. First he gobbled the pears and wolfed down the peaches. He stopped for a moment to catch his breath, and then he devoured the grapes. Next he chomped on the apples, and finally, he nibbled the cherries. He ate all day long and well into the night. At last he could eat no more and lay down to sleep under one of the apple trees.

In the morning the fox had a leisurely breakfast of peaches and grapes, and then decided it was time to return to his den. He put his head through the hole in the wall and found to his great surprise that his body would not follow. He had eaten too much and again he was too fat to get through!

Just then he heard voices coming from the outside of the wall. It was the gardener and the wealthy merchant discussing the fruit, and they agreed that it would be best to harvest it in six days' time.

"If I am still here after six more days, I will be killed," thought the fox. "I must get out the same way I got in. Again I will have to fast until I am thin."

Thus he starved himself for five more miserable days. It was especially difficult with so much ripe fruit within easy reach, but he was willing to suffer in order to live.

At last he was skinny once again and was able to squeeze through the small hole, but oh, how unhappy he was that he had to return home so hungry.

The Squire's Bride

A Norwegian Tale

LONG ago in Norway, there lived a wealthy squire named Jensen. He owned the largest farm in the valley and had money in the bank. He should have been happy, but because he was old and lived alone, he wasn't.

Thus he decided to marry the young daughter of his poor neighbor, Farmer Patterson. Her name was Ingrid, and she was the prettiest, as well as the most stubborn, girl in the valley.

The next day the old squire walked to his neighbor's barnyard and found the girl feeding the chickens.

"I've been thinking of getting married, my dear Ingrid, that is, if you'll agree."

"Me, marry you?" laughed Ingrid. "Don't be foolish, you're much too old for me."

Now Squire Jensen was used to having his own way. He went to her father and said, "Neighbor Patterson, you owe me three hundred kroner and two cows. If you will convince your daughter to marry me, I'll pay for the wedding and forget the debt. If not, I'll buy your farm out from under you."

"Don't you worry, Squire," said the

farmer. "Ingrid will see reason soon enough." He was very worried about his farm, and thought that he could talk his daughter into the marriage.

"No! No! No!" cried Ingrid. "I will not marry that old man! Even if he owned every farm in the valley, I would not be his bride!"

The next day Farmer Patterson explained to Squire Jensen, "My daughter is thinking it over. She will soon come to the right decision."

"She must decide by tomorrow, or your debt becomes due," the squire declared.

Since Farmer Patterson didn't have the money or the cows, he had to tell the squire that Ingrid had at last agreed, and only hope that she would change her mind before the wedding day.

On the next day, he said to the squire, "Ingrid will marry you, but you must keep the wedding dress and crown at your house. Invite all the neighbors, and when the parson is ready, send for my daughter. Have the women help her dress, and you'll be married before she can change her mind."

The squire's servants cleaned and baked all week long in order to have everything ready. When the guests and the parson were assembled, the squire sent one of his farm boys to find Farmer Patterson.

"My master sent me to fetch what you two talked about," said the boy to Ingrid's father.

Farmer Patterson crossed his fingers for luck and said, "She is down in the hayfield, lad."

The boy ran to the hayfield and found Ingrid feeding a little bay mare. "I've come for what the squire and your father talked about."

Ingrid guessed what was happening and

said, "I hate to give her up, but if the squire wants my mare, then he shall have her."

The boy rode the horse to the back door of the Squire's mansion, leaped to the ground and ran inside.

"Is she here?" the squire asked anxiously.

The boy nodded.

"Then take her up the back stairs to the large bedroom."

"But why?" asked the confused boy.

"Don't ask any questions! Have the farmhands help you if she is troublesome."

It took several of the men to push and pull the frightened mare up the stairs and into the bedroom. On the bed lay a beautiful wedding dress and crown.

The boy ran back to the squire and said, "We have her upstairs, Master."

"Send the women in to help her dress. Ask no questions and tell the women to be quick about it."

The women giggled when they heard the order, but supposed that it was all a joke to make the guests laugh. They had to split the dress down the back and drape it over the reluctant horse and tie the crown on her head. When she was ready, the boy ran to tell the squire.

"Bring her down and the wedding will begin," said the squire proudly.

There was a terrible clatter of hoofs on the stairs and the squire's mouth fell open when the bride, looking very much like a horse, appeared. The guests began to laugh and they laughed until they cried.

Old Squire Jensen became the laughing stock of the valley and never again did he ask a young girl to be his bride.

The Alligator and the Jackal

An East Indian Tale

ONCE a hungry jackal heard that an elephant had died on the other side of the wide river. He wanted to cross the river and feast on elephant meat, but he couldn't swim.

As he walked along the riverbank he saw an old and rather large alligator sleeping in the sun. The jackal ran to a safe place and cried: "Wake up, mighty alligator! Time is short and your bride awaits!"

The alligator opened one eye and then the other. "My bride?"

"Oh yes," said the jackal. "There is a beautiful young maiden in the village on the other side of the river. She would make a splendid bride for you. Why not ask for her hand?"

"How would I do that, friend jackal?"

"It is easy," said the jackal. "Simply carry me across the river on your broad back, and I'll make all the arrangements."

The alligator agreed and swam across the river with the jackal on his back. When they reached the opposite side, the jackal leaped onto the sand and said, "Return at sunset to carry me home and I'll tell you of my success."

Then the jackal ran into the jungle and

found the dead elephant. He ate all day long and was stuffed when the sun began to set. The alligator was waiting for him at the riverbank.

"When will she marry me?" he asked.

"I told her how strong and handsome you are," said the jackal, "and she was quite willing, and so was her mother and her brother. But her father wasn't home, so we will have to come again tomorrow to get his permission."

The next morning the alligator gave the jackal another ride across the river, and returned for him at sunset. The jackal, who had feasted all day on the elephant carcass, was waiting for him.

"Did her father agree?" asked the alligator anxiously.

"He wants to think it over," said the jackal. "He told me to return tomorrow for the answer. But the girl is truly in love with you and is eager for the marriage!"

And so it went. Each day the jackal invented a new delay and thus had an excuse to return to the other side of the river to dine on the elephant. When he had finally eaten the last of the meat he rode home on the alligator's back, telling him tales of the girl's undying love for him.

When they arrived at the riverbank the jackal leaped from his back and ran into the jungle. He then laughed long and loud, and cried, "Alligator, I have unfortunate news. Since you are really so stupid and ugly, the girl doesn't want to marry you after all. But I want to thank you for the many rides across the river. You make an excellent ferry boat!"

The alligator was angry at being tricked and wanted revenge. After thinking about it for weeks, he came up with an idea.

He crawled into the deep jungle and found the jackal's den. He stretched out near the entrance, became stiff in all of his joints, and lay there without moving. He was pretending to be dead.

Before long, the jackal returned and saw the alligator. He stayed behind a tree and began to talk out loud to himself.

"Oh my, there is a dead alligator near my den. But wait, is he really dead? Dead alligators always curve their tails to the left, and this tail sticks out straight."

The alligator slowly curved his tail to the left.

The jackal laughed and ran into the jungle. From a safe distance he called, "Thank you alligator, for showing me that you are still alive and still very, very stupid!"

The Court Jester

A Polish Tale

ONCE upon a time, an old jester entertained the royalty of a small kingdom. Joseph was his name, and when he was young, all of the court enjoyed his silly antics. The King and Queen and the lords and ladies laughed for hours at his funny jokes and tricks. But now that he was old, his jokes fell flat and he received more yawns than applause.

Sadly, the King summoned Joseph. "My faithful clown," he said, "you have made us merry for many years, but the time has come for you to retire. I have had a small cottage built for you and your good wife, Anna. I will also give you a small bag of gold, and wish you peace and comfort in your old age."

A tear rolled down Joseph's cheek, "As you wish, Your Majesty." He removed his colorful clown suit and funny cap with the long ears and little bells for the last time. Then, with Anna at his side and his head held high, he walked to his new home.

The small bag of gold was soon empty and Joseph and Anna grew hungry. They were too proud to beg, and because of their old age, no one would give them work. Soon they were desperate.

One day Joseph took his jester's rattle down from the shelf to dust it off, and an idea popped into his old head. "Anna," he said, "go to the Queen and tell her that I died in my sleep. Be sure to cry and carry on like a grieved wife should."

The queen was shocked when she heard the sad news, for she had always liked the jester. "Poor Anna," she said, "please take this purse of gold. It will help to give our dear old joker a proper burial, and you can live on whatever is left."

Anna counted the gold as she walked home, and laughed out loud. One hundred gold pieces!

Joseph, too, was pleased, but added, "Now good wife, it is your turn to die. I will go to the King tomorrow and tell him the sad news."

Joseph put on a fine performance of sorrow and loss, and the King was touched.

"My dear old clown, how sorry I am for you. Take this small chest of gold and try to make a happy life for yourself."

Upon his return, Joseph found that the King had given him 300 pieces of gold. "Now we are rich, Anna! No longer will we starve."

Meanwhile, the King and the Queen were having an argument. The Queen said that the old joker had died, but the King explained that it was Anna, the jester's wife, who was dead. Finally the Queen insisted on going to the jester's cottage to prove that she was right. The King agreed.

Joseph heard the approach of the royal coach and said, "Quickly Anna, let us lie down and pretend to be dead. You sprinkle some white flour on our faces, and I'll cover us with a sheet."

The King and Queen walked into the cottage and saw the old couple lying side by side. The Queen dabbed her eyes and the King blew his nose. Then the King said, "Joseph must have died from grief, soon after Anna."

"No," said the Queen. "Anna must have died from grief, just after Joseph."

"But Anna died first!" exclaimed the King.

"Joseph died first!" replied the Queen.

"Excuse me," said Joseph as he sat up in the bed. "My wife died just before I did, but of course, I was already dead."

The King laughed long and loud, and then said, "Explain this foolishness to me, jester."

Joseph explained how poverty had forced him to play his last trick, and the King and Queen agreed that the old court jester and his wife should keep all of the gold that they had been given.

And so it was that Joseph and Anna lived in comfort until the end of their days.

Pandora's Box

A Greek Tale

THERE once was a time, long, long ago, in which trouble did not exist in the world. Everyone was healthy, happy and loving. The golden sun shone bright each day, and wild flowers were always in bloom. The earth was a garden of joy.

A young woman named Pandora lived in this garden and she, like all the others, was beautiful and full of laughter. She also had a quality that was hers alone, and that was curiosity. If Pandora saw a closet, she opened the door to peek inside. If she found a pot on the fire, she lifted the lid to see what was cooking. If she met a stranger, she asked many questions to find out as much as possible about him. It seemed as though her curiosity was never satisfied.

One day Pandora came home from playing in the meadow, and found a strange and beautiful box sitting near the door.

"Where did this come from?" she asked her husband whose name was Epimetheus.

"A man carrying a staff with two snakes twisting around it, brought it. He also had little wings on his heels and on his cap," answered Epimetheus.

"That was Mercury, the messenger of the gods, and he must have brought the box for me. I can't wait to see what is inside!"

"No!" exclaimed Epimetheus. "The messenger said that it was not to be opened under any circumstances."

"But how will I know if it's for me or not, unless I open it?" Pandora asked.

"Forget about the box," said her husband. "Let's go to the vegetable garden and gather our food for this evening's meal."

"No, Epimetheus, you go on alone," sighed Pandora. "I'll just stay here and rest."

"As soon as her husband was gone, Pandora began to examine the strange box. It was made of beautifully carved wood. A gold cord with a complex knot was the only thing that held it shut. She shook the box to see if it rattled, and to her great surprise heard the pleading of tiny voices coming from inside: "Help! Let us out! Please Pandora, untie the knot! Oh hurry, dear Pandora, hurry and open the box!"

She could stand no more. She had to know what was inside. Pandora untied the golden knot and slowly opened the lid to peek inside. Instantly a black cloud filled the room and hundreds of horrible, little insect-like creatures flew out, shrieking and laughing with cruel voices!

Just then, Epimetheus rushed into the house and was stung by several of the little demons. He screamed and Pandora let the lid fall back in place. But it was too late, for all the troubles on earth had been set free. Sickness, pain, jealousy, hate, lies and all the other evils flew out of the house and into the world.

Then Pandora heard another little voice

coming from inside the box, a voice sweeter than the others. "Please let me out too, Pandora, for I bring help."

She opened the lid once more and a bright light came from inside the box, chasing the dark cloud away. A tiny creature with golden wings flew up and touched Epimetheus on the shoulder where he had been stung, and the pain that he suffered vanished.

"Who are you?" asked Pandora.

"My name is Hope, and as long as there is trouble in the world, I will be there to comfort all of humankind."

Close the Door!

An American Tale

THERE once lived a husband and wife who were stubborn. While having supper one night a strong gust of wind blew the cottage door wide open.

"Husband," said the woman, "get up and close the door before the wind blows our meat and potatoes onto the floor."

"You close it, wife. I worked in the fields all day and I'm tired."

"I worked all day as well," said the wife. "You close it."

"My work is harder than yours and I want YOU to close the door!" yelled the man.

"No!" said the wife. "My work doesn't end at sundown, like yours. You close it!"

"Wife, you are as stubborn as our mule!"

"Husband, you are worse!"

They both knew that neither one would win the argument, so they agreed to be silent. They also agreed that the first to break the silence by speaking would have to close the door against the cold night wind. They remained silent for hours, and when it was time to go to bed, they crawled under the covers without a word.

A thief who was both cold and hungry

happened by. He thought it strange to find the door wide open, a cold fireplace, and the man and woman in bed with their eyes open wide and their mouths shut tight.

"Good evening," said the thief, "could you spare a crust of bread for a hungry man?"

Absolute silence was the reply.

"What's that you say?" asked the thief. "Help myself to all the food I want?"

He wasted no time in placing all the food in the house on the table cloth and wrapping it up into a large bundle.

"And now, would you happen to have an old coat to spare, to help keep the chill from my bones?" asked the thief.

The silence continued.

"Why thank you, I will take whatever I can use," said the thief, and he emptied the closets and made a second bundle.

"Before I leave, my friends, could I trouble you for a coin or two? What's that? Take all I can find? You're too kind!"

The thief searched throughout the cottage and found all the money that had been hidden away. Thinking that he must have a little more fun with this foolish couple, he went to the fireplace and filled his hands with soot.

"Here is a little gift for you, my quiet friends," said the thief, and he smeared the soot all over the woman's face.

Neither husband nor wife said a word.

The thief picked up the bundles of food and clothing and, with his pockets heavy with coins, walked out of the cottage.

The man and woman lay in bed the rest of the night without speaking. The door to their cottage stood wide open.

The birds sang a cheery morning song as the sun rose in the eastern sky. The couple sat up in bed and the man looked at his wife.

"Wife, your face is all black!" he exclaimed.

"Husband, you spoke first. Get up and close the door!"

About the Author

Pleasant deSpain, professional storyteller, writer and television personality, was born in Denver, Colorado, in 1943 and has been teaching and performing most of his life. He has taught oral interpretation, readers theatre, and communication courses at the University of Massachusetts, Colorado University, and the University of Washington. He has also taught language arts, drama, and storytelling in the Seattle Public Schools. In 1975, Pleasant left teaching and began his storytelling career. Since then he has devoted himself to storytelling as an entertaining art form. His programs for all ages consist of folk and fairy tales, myths, legends, and original stories designed to captivate and nourish the imaginations of young and old alike.

In April, 1975, Pleasant deSpain was officially proclaimed "Seattle's Resident Storyteller," by then-mayor Wes Uhlman. In September of 1977, he began his popular weekly television show, "Pleasant Journeys," on KING-TV, Seattle, as well as a weekly story-column in *The Seattle Times*.

In addition to his television program, the "circuit rider of the imagination" performs regularly at elementary, junior and senior high schools, libraries, colleges, theatres, churches, hospitals, and lecture halls throughout the Pacific Northwest.

About the Illustrator

Kirk Lyttle is a free-lance illustrator and cartoonist from Seattle, Washington. His talent surfaced at an early age, and though he exhibited a rare facility for rational behavior, it was inevitable that despite all, he was destined to become an artist.

Kirk spent three years on the staff of the University of Washington *Daily* drawing editorial cartoons. After graduating, he worked at *The Seattle Times* as an artist. Kirk has also illustrated "Mother Goose Flipped" by Sammi Andirsen.